The Adventures of Sammy
The Squirrel

The Adventures Of Sammy The Squirrel
Copyright © 2026 by "Azra"

DEDICATION

To the precious little hearts I've had the honor of nurturing over the years-your laughter, your love, and your light have filled my world in ways words can hardly capture. You've left footprints on my heart that time will never erase. This book is but a small reflection of the countless lessons you've gifted me and the boundless joy you've brought into my life. You are, and always will be, my greatest inspiration

Once upon a time, in a big, green forest where the trees stood tall and the air was filled with the sweet scent of pine, there lived Sammy the Squirrel. Sammy was not your everyday squirrel. No, he was special. His fur was the color of rich chestnuts, and his eyes sparkled with an adventurous gleam. What set Sammy apart from the other squirrels was his keen curiosity. He couldn't resist exploring every nook and cranny of the forest, always eager to discover something new.

One sunny morning, as the golden rays of the sun filtered through the emerald leaves, Sammy was hopping from tree to tree, his bushy tail bouncing with each joyful leap. Suddenly, his sharp eyes caught a glimmer near a bush - something shiny and mysterious..

As Sammy approached the bush, his heart raced with excitement. There was a tiny, sparkling key in the middle of the leaves. Sammy's eyes widened, and a surge of curiosity rushed through him. What could this key unlock? His adventurous spirit took hold, and Sammy knew he had to find out.

With the tiny key gripped in his delicate paws, Sammy ran through the forest with his tail trailing behind him like a fluffy banner. When he went deeper into the woods, Sammy encountered Oliver, a wise old owl with feathers like gray velvet and big, round glasses perched on his beak. With a twinkle in his eyes, Oliver sensed Sammy's excitement and beckoned him closer.

"Ah, young Sammy," hooted Oliver, "I see you have found a key to the mysteries of the enchanted forest. Take heed, my friend, for great wonders await those who dare to unlock the secrets hidden within."

With his wide eyes and eagerness, Sammy listened intently as Oliver shared tales of magical creatures and hidden treasure. His stories created fascination that fueled Sammy's curiosity even more.

With Oliver's wise words echoing in his mind, Sammy pressed on. He stumbled upon a hidden door, covered in vines and sheltered in the whispers of the wind. Standing silent and forgotten for years, the door seemed to summon Sammy with a promise of extraordinary discoveries.

With a deep breath, Sammy inserted the key into the lock, an
as he turned it, a soft click resonated through the air. The
door creaked open, revealing a world beyond Sammy's wildes
dreams. Colors more colorful than he can find in the forest
surround him, and the air buzzed with an energy that spok
of magic

In this magical world, meadows of candy-colored flowers stretched as far as the eye could see, and the sky filled with the type and color of butterflies unseen in the ordinary forest. Sammy met Rosie, a fluffy rabbit with ears as pink, and Remy, a raccoon with mischievous in his eyes. They became fast friends, and together, they went deeper into the wonderland.

Their journey led them to Penny, a pixie with a twinkle in her eye and a soft laugh that sparkled like fairy dust. With a mischievous grin, Penny guided them to the center of the magical forest, where dreams were said to come alive.

At the center of the forest, they discovered a pond that sparkled with a silvery glow. The pond, said to reflect the dreams of those who believed, became a source for Sammy, Rosie, and Remy to make their wishes come true. To their surprise, each wish turned into glowing butterflies, fluttering around them with joy. The friends giggled with delight, realizing that the magic of the enchanted forest responded to their hopes and dreams.

But, as every tale must have its challenge, a grumpy gnome named Grizzle appeared, casting a shadow of doubt over their newfound happiness. Grizzle has a mark on his wrinkled face, and he tries to shake the belief of all three friends in magic. With their belief undeterred, Sammy, Rosie, and Remy stood firm. They did not think badly of him, but tried to make Grizzle believe in magic as well. Grizzle saw their friendship shining brighter than the moon above.

As they continued their adventure, they came across a wise old tree that told them tales of courage and bravery. Inspired by the ancient wisdom of the tree, Sammy found a courage within himself that he never knew existed. With his newfound bravery, the friends faced the final challenge of the magical forest.

They come across a swirling vortex that was destroying
the surroundings of the forest as well. However, they all
stood strong, holding each other with paws in paws. They
ensured each other that this vortex would pass soon.

With their dedication, they all started to run around the vortex in the opposite direction. Other creatures from around also joined them. After some time, as they all gained speed, the vortex started to disappear.

With the enchanted forest saved and their friendship stronger than ever, Sammy, Rosie, and Remy bid farewell to the magical creatures they had met along the way. They all learned the lessons of courage, friendship, and the extraordinary power of belief.

Back in their ormal woodland, Sammy shared the tales of
their extraordinary adventure with other animals. The
woodland creatures, captivated by the magic of Sammy's
story, felt a new found sense of wonder and possibility in
their hearts.

As the sun dipped below the horizon, casting a warm glow over the forest, Sammy looked up at the twinkling stars. The same stars that had witnessed their magical journey. He knew that the magic they experienced would forever be a part of their hearts. With a satisfied sigh, Sammy sat down in his cozy nest.

The END